LOOK AGAIN!

TANA HOBAN

MACMILLAN PUBLISHING COMPANY
New York
COLLIER MACMILLAN PUBLISHERS
London

The photographs in this book were taken with two
single-lens-reflex cameras: the Beseler Topcon RE Super D
(35mm), using 58mm, 135mm and 85/210mm electric zoom
lenses; and the Hasselblad 1000 F (2¼″ x 2¼″), using
40mm, 80mm and 135mm lenses. Various close-up lenses
were used with both cameras. The films used were Plus-X Pan
and Tri-X, developed in Ethol UFG and printed on Varigam
paper in Dektol solution.

Macmillan Publishing Company
866 Third Avenue, New York, New York 10022
Collier Macmillan Canada, Inc.
ISBN 0-02-744050-8
Library of Congress catalog card number: 72-127469

16   15   14   13   12   11

To E., who taught me to see